T0131725

Ricky Ice

A Ninja's Destiny

Landon Noisette

ISBN: Softcover 978-1-7960-3440-0
EBook 978-1-7960-3439-4

Print information available on the last page

Rev. date: 06/24/2019

To order additional copies of this book, contact:
Xlibris
1-888-795-4274
www.Xlibris.com
Orders@Xlibris.com

1:00 AM
Ricky wake up its time to train.
Snore!
Nooo I'm so tired that I can't even move anymore.
Now!
Ricky wake up now or face the horrible consequences.

2
I bet you don't even have a consequence.

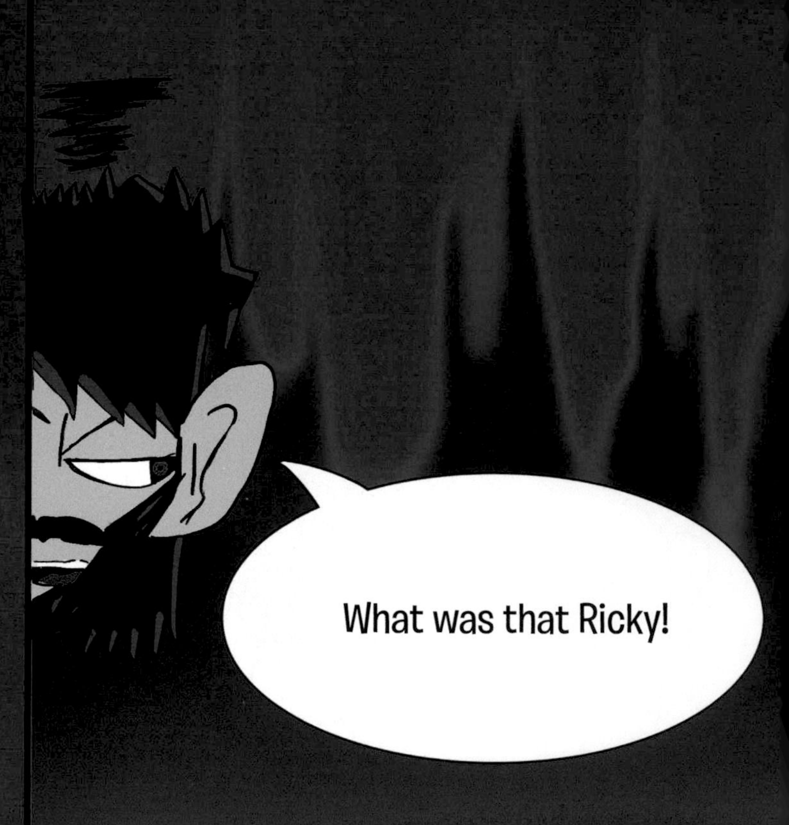
What was that Ricky!

Nothing. Nothing at all!

Anyways what happened to breakfast I'm starving.

* -A genin is a lower ranked ninja
*- A "D" rank mission is a mission that only a genin go on.

Hey Ricky you better not be sleeping or else!
Ricky!
Snore snore!

That's it electric water style jutsu

Ahhhhhhhhh.
Cough

What was that for!
Because you were sleeping!
Plus you might want to get ready for school!
Aw shoot I got to go.

6
I gotta go now
Wait before you go you have to study 500 jutsu's in 5 styles in this book
Whaaaa aaaaaaa aaaaaat!
I'm proud of you son
Wait we also will fight when you come back.
Meet me back here when you're done

Yawn!
This book is so boring.
I could go into my dads office and learn a bunch of awesome jutsu's

?
Hmm but how.
Yes! this could work!
Maybe I could make clones with my clone jutsu the first clone could fight Dad. The second could pack my bags for school.
Let's put this plan into action!

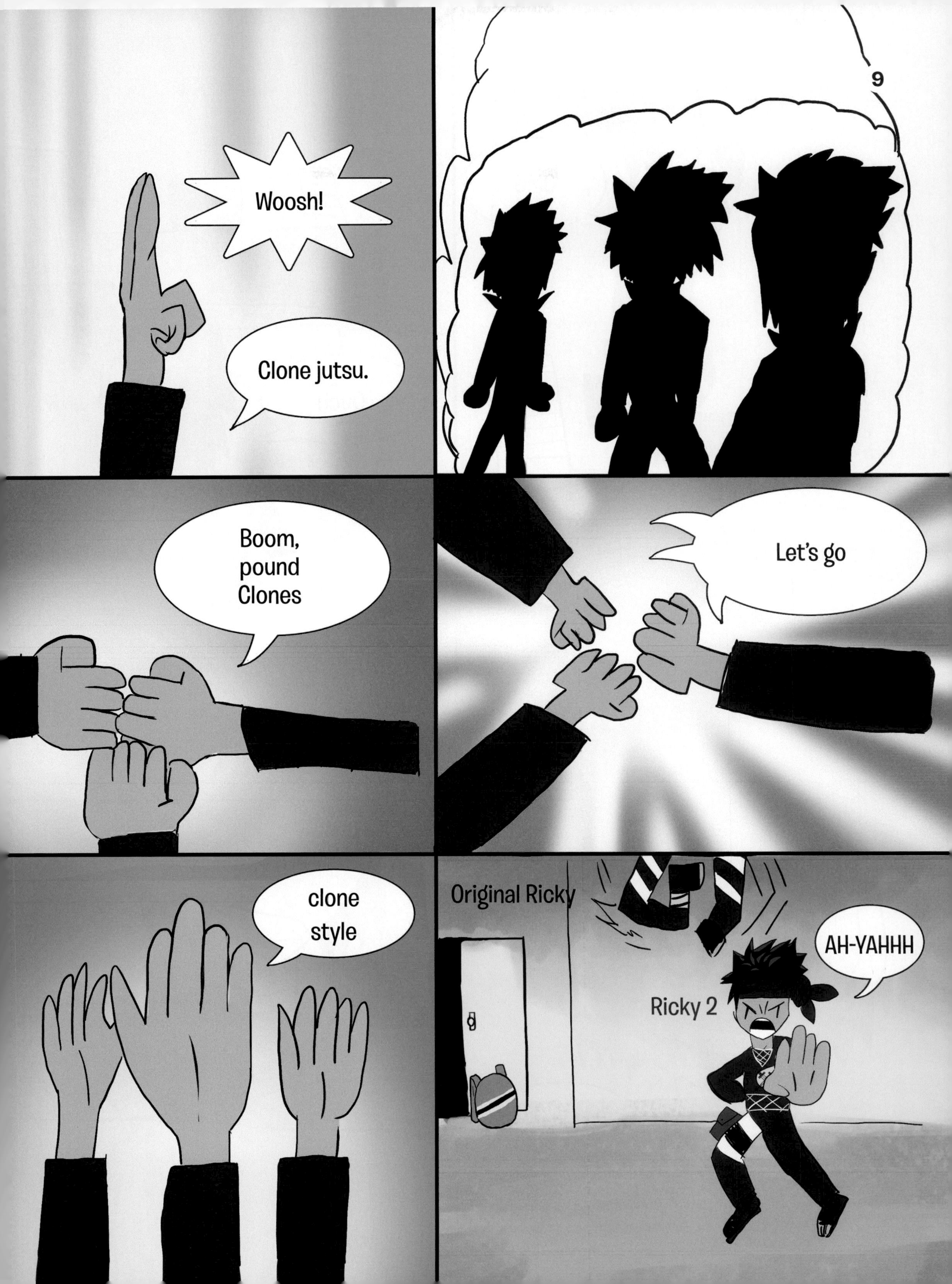
Woosh!
Clone jutsu.
Boom, pound Clones
Let's go
clone style
Original Ricky
AH-YAHHH
Ricky 2

OMG
Ouch
Now let's get studying

Original Ricky stop fooling around
Ok jeez Ricky 2.

Oh yeah I gotta find a Justu for Ricky 2

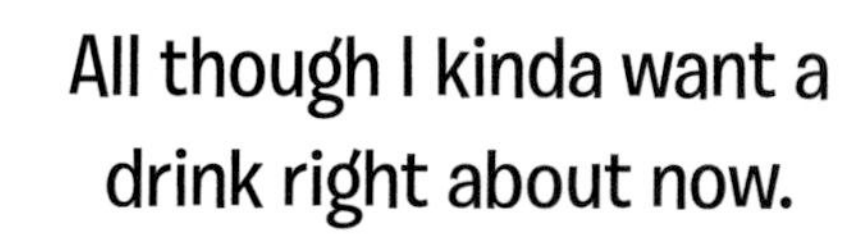
All though I kinda want a drink right about now.

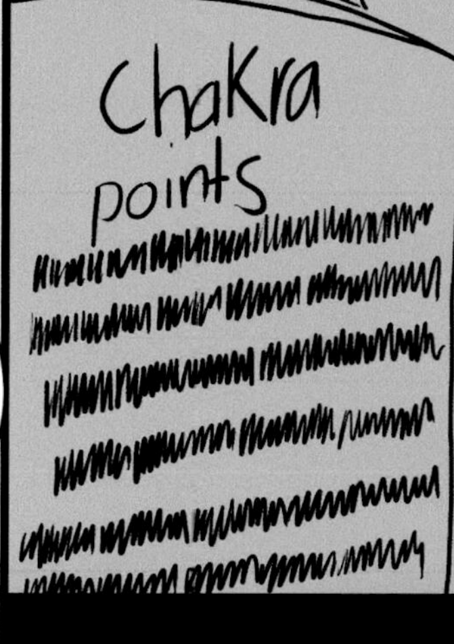
Chakra points
Resuscitation Jutsu

All right Ricky focus

Ricky 2 I have an idea on how we could beat Dad.

13
Tell me I'm dying to know because he's kicking my butt right now
I see. Do you have a *shriken with you?
Uh yeah. I do.
-* shriken- a ninja tool

Throw
it now

Ok Jeez.

Hope this
works

Nice try
but you
are too
slow.

Lightning wind
shriken fortex

5 minutes later

Printed in the United States
By Bookmasters